D1394925

# BEN AND THE SPIDER GATE

# BEN
# AND THE
# SPIDER GATE

*Best wishes*

Angela Fish

*Angela Fish*

Book Guild Publishing
Sussex, England

First published in Great Britain in 2015 by
The Book Guild Ltd
The Werks
45 Church Road
Hove, BN3 2BE

Typesetting in Palatino by
Nat-Type, Cheshire

Printed in Great Britain by
CPI Group (UK) Ltd, Croydon, CR0 4YY

A catalogue record for this book is available from
The British Library.

ISBN 978 1 910508 25 1

# Contents

1    Ben Meets Lox        1

2    Gran Tells Ben About Autumn        9

3    The Birthday Wish        17

4    The Adventure Game        22

5    Following The Magpies        28

6    The Woods        33

7    Scoot's Search        39

8    The Final Piece        44

9    The Spider Wizard's Magic        49

# 1

## *Ben Meets Lox*

There was once a boy called Ben, who lived in a little house with his mum, dad and grandmother, and a dog called Scoot. Ben liked his house. He had his own bedroom and out of the window he could see the back garden. Ben loved the garden. It was his favourite place in the whole world.

The garden had a path right down the middle and a shed near the back door. Dad grew vegetables on one side of the path, and on the other side there was a lawn and two big trees at the far end. There was a tall hedge all the way around the outside of the garden, with a little gate into the back lane. Each spring the robins would come and build their nest in the hedge. Ben used to listen to them chirping to each other. He was so excited when their eggs were hatched. The baby birds made such a lot of noise and he really wanted to see them.

'They'll be frightened, Ben,' his dad told him. 'They're so tiny and you'd look like a giant to them.' So Ben waited and it wasn't long before he could see mum and dad robin flying in and out of the hedge looking for food for the chicks. Every evening Ben used to help his dad to fill up the bird feeders which hung on the side of the shed. From his bedroom window he could watch the robins, sparrows and lots of other birds pecking for the seeds. His mother was teaching him the names of the birds but he couldn't always remember all of them. When the little robins started to fly, Ben was sad because he knew they'd soon move away.

'Never mind, Ben,' his mum told him, 'they'll be back next year.' He knew she was right but a whole year seemed like such a long time.

One day, near the end of the summer holidays, Ben was playing in the garden with Scoot. Scoot was a black and white dog and he was very clever. Ben's dad had a special whistle and he'd trained Scoot to come to him whenever the dog heard it. At the start of the holidays Ben's dad had taught Ben how to use the whistle and he tried it now.

'Good boy, Scoot! You're so smart. Let's play ball now.'

Even though Scoot was little, he could run very fast. Ben threw the ball high in the air and Scoot jumped up after it and then chased it down the garden path. Ben laughed, then he sat down on the grass and watched Scoot pushing the ball around with his nose. The sun was hot and after a while Scoot lay down in the shade of the garden shed and rested his head on his paws. Ben began to feel sleepy as well and his eyes started to close.

When he opened them again he thought he was still asleep and dreaming. He wasn't a big boy any more, he was a very little boy. He wasn't much bigger than one of the daisies that were growing in the grass! He looked around. Everything looked the same only now it was huge, even Scoot, who was looking at Ben as if he was one of his toys.

Very carefully, Ben crawled towards the path but he stopped when he heard a strange noise. It sounded like someone was crying.

'Who's there?' Ben called out. 'Where are you?'

'I'm over here, on top of the box next to the tree,' came the answer.

Ben jumped and turned around. He rubbed his eyes and stared at the box. That morning it had been just an ordinary shoe box that he kept his toy cars in, but now it looked as big as a garage. On top of the box sat a big spider, but Ben wasn't frightened because the spider looked so sad, and big fat tears were dropping down from his eyes.

'What's the matter?' Ben asked. 'Why are you crying?'

'I've lost something,' the spider sobbed. 'Well, someone stole it, really.'

'Oh no.' Ben moved a little closer. 'Can I help you find it?'

The spider crawled down from the box and looked at Ben. 'Well, maybe. Come and sit over here and I'll tell you about it.' So Ben sat down and the spider began his story.

3

'I am called Lox and I am the guardian of the spider kingdom's gate. It was made many years ago to stop anything coming in to our land. Spiders can pass in and out but only through the gate. I have to make sure that it's guarded at all times but this morning, when I came to check, the night guard was missing and a huge bird was breaking up the gate.'

'A bird?' Ben looked worried. He hoped it wasn't the robins. He hadn't seen them for a while but that didn't mean that they weren't around. 'What kind of bird?'

'What do you mean, what kind?' the spider asked. 'Birds are birds. It looked like that.' He waved one of his legs towards the house and Ben could see an enormous magpie perched on the roof.

'Anyway, I tried to save the gate but he pecked at me so I hid in the grass. I saw him break the gate into three pieces, and then he picked them up in his beak and flew off. I saw one piece fall somewhere near the box but I don't know where he took the others.' Lox began to cry again. Ben patted the leg nearest to him.

'Don't cry,' he said. 'I'll help you. What does the gate look like?'

The spider dried his eyes with his two front legs, then ran through the grass to the back of the box. 'Come on,' he shouted to Ben, 'see if we can find the first piece, then you'll know. It's here somewhere.'

Ben ran after him and together they pushed through the grass and daisies until Lox called out, 'Here. Here it is. Please help me pull it out.' Ben stared. Just at the bottom of one of the trees was a large dandelion and poking out from under its leaves was something that looked very much like part of a spider's web. This wasn't soft and squashy though, it was hard and shiny. It was just like the gates he'd seen at the front of the castle in his story book.

'Pull!' said Lox, and Ben helped him to drag the piece of gate along the path and under the hedge. It was hard work as the piece was nearly as big as Ben. 'Over here.' Lox pointed and Ben could see a cave at the back of the hedge near the fence.

'But who made this gate?' Ben scratched his head. 'Why does it look like a cobweb but it isn't?'

Lox smiled. 'It is a web but it was made here long, long ago by the Spider Queen's workmen. When it was finished and it covered the entrance, the queen's wizard sang a magic song and the web became hard and strong. It's never been broken until now and it's all my fault.'

Ben thought Lox was going to cry again so he said quickly, 'No, it's not. It was the magpie. My gran says that magpies love shiny things. Can't the wizard make a new gate?'

'No,' Lox said. 'The gate-making song only works twice and there's another gate at the far end of the kingdom, so the song can't be sung again.'

'If I help you find the other pieces, can it be fixed together again?' Ben asked.

'Yes, I think so,' Lox said, 'but the wizard's magic will only work until the leaves on the trees fall off.'

Ben thought for a moment. Lox meant autumn, when all the leaves turned red, or orange, or brown before they fell off the trees, but Ben wasn't quite sure when that would be. He'd have to ask Gran. She

knew everything, but how would she be able to see or hear him now that he was so small? He turned to Lox.

'All right. I'll help you but I have to go back to my house now. Call your guards and make them stay here. I'll come back to let you know if I find anything. If I'm bigger than this next time, will you be afraid of me?'

Lox looked at Ben. 'What do you mean – bigger?'

Ben put his hands in his pockets and hopped from foot to foot. 'Well, I'm not usually this small,' he said. 'I don't know what happened to me but if I go back to being big, I promise I won't hurt you when I come back.'

Lox looked a little bit worried but nodded his head. 'All right, but please hurry.'

Ben ran as quickly as he could through the grass. It seemed such a long way now that he was so tiny. When he reached the edge of the grass he had to climb up onto the path. This made him very tired so he sat down for a rest. He closed his eyes and drifted off to sleep. When he woke up, Scoot was licking his hand. Ben stared at Scoot. He wasn't huge at all. Then Ben looked at his own hands and feet and saw that he was back to his normal size.

'Oh, Scoot. I must have been dreaming all the time. Silly me!' he said. 'Come on, time for tea.' Then he threw Scoot's ball towards the back door of the house and they both chased after it.

# 2

## *Gran Tells Ben About Autumn*

Ben opened the kitchen door but he could see that Scoot was pawing and licking at something that was caught in the doormat. 'What have you got there, boy? Let me see.' Scoot wagged his tail but he didn't want to give up his prize and he kept his paw over it. 'Come on, Scoot, show me. You can have a biscuit if you do.' Ben reached inside the kitchen door and took a biscuit from Scoot's bowl. 'Here, Scoot. Here.' Ben offered the treat to Scoot. The dog jumped for it and moved off the mat. Ben poked his fingers through the back of the mat and tried to push out what was stuck there. All of a sudden something popped out onto the floor and Ben picked it up.

'Yuk, Scoot. You slobbered all over it.' Ben made a face and wiped the thing on his trousers and then put it on the palm of his hand. It was small and hard, and looked like a piece of chain or something like that. Once it was dry it began to shine in the sunlight and Ben prodded it with his finger. His eyes opened wide and he sat down suddenly on the doorstep.

'Oh, Scoot! Look what you found. Look.' Scoot pushed his wet nose against Ben's hand and wagged

9

his tail hard. 'It's another piece, Scoot. Another piece of the spider gate.'

Ben ran back down the garden path with Scoot right behind him. When he was near the hedge he lay flat on the ground and crawled towards the spider cave. Now that he was normal size it looked very small. There was no sign of Lox – just two ordinary-looking garden spiders who scuttled away when they saw Ben. He tried calling out quietly, 'Lox, Lox, it's me, Ben. I found another piece. Look!' After a few minutes he knew Lox wasn't coming out, so he put the piece of gate very carefully next to the cave and wriggled away.

'Come on Scoot. Time to go in.' They both ran up the path and into the kitchen where Ben's grandmother was having a cup of tea and reading the newspaper.

'Hello, Ben. What have you been up to? You look as though you could do with a bath.' Gran smiled at him and Ben wondered if he should tell her about Lox and the gate. He thought he would, but maybe later when she read him his bedtime story. Now he wanted to find out more about autumn.

'Gran?'

'Yes, Ben? What is it?'

'When does autumn start?'

'Oh dear, that's a hard question. People usually say that autumn begins near the end of September but there's no exact date, really. Why do you want to know?' Gran smiled at him again.

'I just wanted to know when the leaves change colour and fall off. That is in autumn, isn't it?'

'Yes, that's right, Ben, but they don't all change colour and fall at the same time. Some change quite quickly and others take a lot longer, and then they fall off. There are some that don't change at all. They don't drop their leaves either. They're called evergreens.'

Ben frowned. He didn't know that. He thought that perhaps Lox didn't know either. If some leaves stayed green all year, did that mean they had more time to find the other piece of the gate? Ben didn't know, so he thought he had better try to find the missing piece as soon as possible, just to make sure that the wizard's magic would work.

He knew he had to do it, although it was only a week until school started.

Later, after the family had eaten and Ben had had his bath, his grandmother sat beside him to read him a story.

'What would you like tonight, Ben?' she asked.

Ben thought for a moment then said, 'Can I tell you a story tonight, Gran? A made-up one?'

'Oh, that's a good idea,' Gran nodded, 'but don't make it too long otherwise I shall fall asleep, just like you do when I read to you!'

Ben laughed. Gran was funny but she did know a lot and he liked talking to her. He said that the story was about a boy called Jake and his adventure in a garden. Then he told her all about the things that had happened to him that day. When he had finished, Gran said, 'Well, Ben. That was amazing. What an excellent story. Are you going to tell me the rest of it tomorrow?'

Ben wrinkled his nose. 'I don't know. I'm not sure how it will end yet. I'll tell you when I know.'

'All right. You do that. Now, it's time for sleep.' Gran kissed him goodnight and put out the light. Ben was so tired that he was asleep in minutes.

Every day Ben searched. He looked on the paths, the front lawn, in the flower beds, the vegetable garden and under the hedge. He poked a stick into the drains, under the shed and into the little holes in the trees – but he found nothing. Scoot thought it was great fun and ran around, wagging his tail.

On the night before school started, Ben asked his grandmother to show him on the kitchen calendar when autumn might start. She took a pencil and put a cross on the twenty-first of September.

'About then, I think,' she said, 'but that's only the start, remember. The leaves don't change colour overnight.'

Ben settled down in bed and he tried to sleep, but he kept thinking about Lox and the gate. He'd made a promise to the spider and he really wanted to keep it, but he knew that he wouldn't have much time to search after tomorrow as he didn't come home from school until four o'clock. He would have the weekends, though. He could look all day Saturday and Sunday if his mum or dad didn't need any help with anything. He felt better about that and soon fell asleep.

14

The next day Ben's mum took him to school in the car. On the way they picked up his best friend, Jess. Sometimes Jess came over to play with Ben but she had been staying at her cousin Poppy's house this summer and so Ben hadn't seen her very often.

'Hi, Ben,' Jess grinned at Ben. 'Had a good holiday?'

'Hi, Jess,' Ben grinned back. 'It was all right. What about you?'

They chatted all the way to school and then played in the yard before the bell rang. Inside, they sat together and were soon busy with their sums and drawings. The day seemed to go by very quickly. Ben thought he might tell Jess about Lox, but then he changed his mind. He knew that Jess would want to come and look at the cave but Lox might be afraid or even cross if Ben brought someone else there. After all, it was a kind of secret place, wasn't it? So he decided to keep the secret to himself for a while. If he ever saw Lox again, he could ask him if Jess could come to see the cave door.

That evening, when Ben was ready for bed, he took a pencil and put a cross on the calendar where Gran showed him. That was today. After that he did the same every night. He was allowed to play in the garden for a little while after school but it wasn't really long enough to do much searching. He was also running out of places to look. He wanted to go out into the lane but he knew he wasn't allowed to go there on his own. He would have to wait for his dad to take him, maybe at the weekend.

But when the weekend came it was raining, so all Ben could do was look out of his window. The weather was bad for a whole week and the calendar page was filling up with crosses. When he reached the number twenty-one, Ben rushed outside to look at the leaves. Most of them were still green, but he was worried now that he wasn't going to find the last piece of the gate in time.

# 3

## *The Birthday Wish*

Two weeks later, on a Friday when Ben came home from school, he could see that the leaves on the big trees in his garden were turning yellow. He started to cry, but then remembered that it was his birthday the next day and that he'd be having a party with a birthday cake. The weather looked as if it was going to be fine, so he thought he'd still have time to search some more.

That night, Gran told him about the words that he had to say before he blew all the candles out and made a wish.

'Remember, Ben, your wish won't come true unless you say the magic words. Come on, one more try.'

Ben said the words and Gran told him that he was a clever lad. He liked that. He thought hard about his wish, but he had two in mind and couldn't decide between them.

'Gran,' he said, 'if we light the candles a second time, can I have another wish?'

Gran laughed. 'No, cheeky! Just the one, so make it a good one. Now, go to sleep and it will soon be morning.'

When Ben woke up the sun was shining and he could hear the birds calling to each other in the garden. He jumped out of bed when he heard the clatter of the letterbox. The postman had been! He ran downstairs and his mum was in the hallway.

'Look Ben, lots of cards, all for you, and there are more in the kitchen. Now go back upstairs and put on your slippers and dressing gown, please.'

Ben went back to his room and did what his mum had asked, then he ran down to the kitchen. The table was laid for breakfast but on his plate were lots of cards, and on his chair were presents from his family. They clapped and cheered when he came into the kitchen and shouted, 'Happy Birthday, Ben!'

Ben opened the envelopes and ripped off the wrapping paper and said 'Thank you' to everyone. Mum and Dad had bought him trainers, and a computer game about a boy who lived in a castle. The boy made friends with a dragon and they had to go on lots of adventures. Gran gave Ben a backpack and torch, and a big book all about birds, as well as a red notebook and pencil. He couldn't stop smiling.

At three o'clock that afternoon his friends began to arrive. For their birthdays, lots of them had had parties in the new burger bar in town, and Mum said that maybe next time Ben could do that. Today they were having a barbecue in the garden and Dad had set up the picnic tables outside as well. Ben and his friends played football on the grass while Dad was cooking and then they all sat down to eat.

Soon it was time for the cake. Gran carried it out and Ben jumped up and down. His cake was shaped like a castle and there were seven silver candles on top. Mum and Gran had made it and Ben could see that the front gate was exactly like Lox's. This was the time to decide which wish to choose. Should he wish that he could find the last piece of the gate, or should he wish that autumn didn't come at all this year?

'Come on, Ben. Time for the candles.' Dad lit them and Ben took a deep breath.

'Don't forget the words, Ben,' Gran reminded him, 'the magic ones.'

Ben shook his head. He'd nearly forgotten.

'Red, orange, yellow, green, purple, blue.
Please make my birthday wish come true.'

He took another big breath in and blew as hard as he could. Five candles went out right away but two of the flames just wobbled. Ben puffed even harder and the two lights went out.

'Hooray, hooray!' Everyone clapped and sang 'Happy Birthday to Ben'.

'So what did you wish for?' Jess poked him in the side.

'Can't tell you, or it won't come true,' Ben said.

'Well, will you tell me if it does come true, then?' Jess asked.

'Yes, all right.' Ben smiled. He'd made his choice.

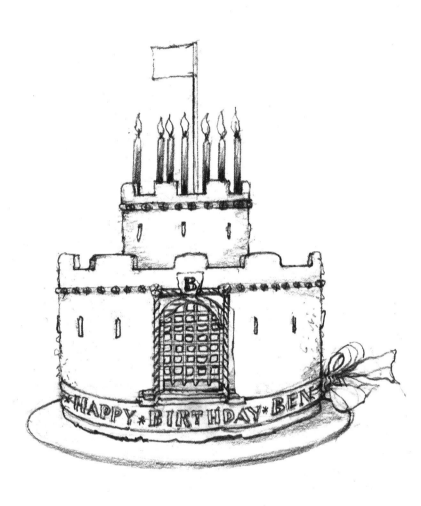

He was going to find the last piece of the gate in the next two weeks. He was. He really was.

Later that night, when Ben was in bed, his gran asked him if he was ready to finish his made-up story.

Ben shook his head. 'Not yet, Gran, but soon.'

'All right. Just tell me when you're ready.' Gran turned off the light.

Ben began to plan how to search in the lane and woods. He would have to do a small patch at a time but he had no idea where to start and how far he would have to look. He was really worried now.

# 4

## *The Adventure Game*

At school the next day Ben told Jess all about his new computer game and how his dad had helped him to put his name into it so that the boy in the game was called Ben. Then he'd shown him how to move the people and things about. Jess thought it sounded like good fun.

'Can I play it as well the next time I come over?' she asked.

'Yes,' Ben told her. 'Maybe your mum can bring you on Saturday.'

Ben liked it when Jess came to his house. There were always lots of games to play in the garden, or inside if the weather was bad. When Ben's mum met them after school, Ben asked if Jess could come over on Saturday and his mum said that was fine as long as Jess's mother agreed. When they arrived at Jess's house her mother said that it was all right and that she would bring Jess over at about eleven o'clock.

On Friday night Ben asked his dad if they could go into the lane on Saturday to do some more training with Scoot, because Jess would like to see how well Scoot was doing. He also thought that he might be able to do some searching for the last piece of the spider gate, but he didn't say anything about that. Dad said that as long as it wasn't raining they could go into the lane with him. The next morning it was pouring with rain and Ben was sad when he looked out of his window. When he went downstairs, there was even more bad news.

'Sorry, Ben,' Dad said, 'but Mum and I have to go into town today. I've broken my glasses and I can't drive without them. Gran will stay here with you so Jess can still come over. The weather isn't good enough to take Scoot training today anyway, but we'll go tomorrow if it's dry. Shall I set up the computer for you?'

Ben nodded. He had really wanted to go outside today. He didn't think he had much more time before his wish ran out. He had to find the last piece of the gate and he had no idea where to start looking. The lane and the woods were so big.

'Cheer up, Ben!' Mum tickled him under his chin and gave him a big hug. 'I'm sure Jess and you will have a great time together. If you ask Gran nicely she might make you something special to eat. We'll be back as soon as we can, I promise.'

Ben smiled at his mother and, after breakfast, he went to the door to wave them goodbye, then he went back up to his room to wait for Jess. He played with his toy cars and then he drew some pictures of birds in the notebook that Gran had given him for his birthday. He heard a sound outside the window and looked out. Two magpies were sitting on a branch of the big tree at the end of the garden. They were making a lot of noise about something but Ben couldn't see what it was. Then they flew to the top of the garden shed and Ben saw that one of them had a piece of bread in its beak. The other one was trying to steal it and they seemed to be arguing. Ben laughed. He loved their black and white feathers, and Dad had shown him in the bird book that, if he looked closely, he could see that there was also some green in their tail feathers. Ben watched for a little while longer, then one of them flew away quickly and the other followed. They flew towards the woods and he lost sight of them.

The doorbell rang and Gran called up to him that Jess had arrived. They had some milk and biscuits and then settled down to play the computer game. Jess loved it. Ben showed her how he had made the boy in the game meet the dragon and how many adventures they had been on. Jess had a go and said that she'd like to have the same game for her birthday.

'It's really good, Ben.' Jess told him. 'Wouldn't it be great if we could do all the things like the boy in the game? You know, go exploring and finding treasure and things like that.'

Ben nodded. 'Mmmm. Yes it would. If it stops raining later we could pretend that the shed is a castle and go exploring in the garden, if you like?'

'Oh, yes please!' Jess clapped her hands. 'We can pretend that the path is the moat around the castle and that the gate in the hedge is the way into the dragon's cave.'

Ben jumped off the chair. 'Let's see what the weather's like now, then we can ask Gran if we can go out.' They both ran into the kitchen and Ben opened the back door. The rain had stopped and the sun was trying to peep out from behind the clouds.

'Gran! Gran! Where are you?' Ben shouted.

'I'm here, Ben, in the hallway. The newspaper has only just arrived. It's really late today. What's the matter?' Gran ruffled his hair.

'Can Jess and I go out in the garden to play? It's stopped raining. Please?'

Gran thought for a moment. 'Well, as long as you put on your boots and wrap up warmly, I think that should be all right. Don't sit on the wet grass, and you must come back in if it starts raining again, though. What are you going to do?'

'We're going to play exploring, like in the computer game that Mum and Dad bought me,' Ben told her.

'Oh. You'll need supplies then?' Gran asked.

'What do you mean, Gran?' Ben looked puzzled.

'Well, all explorers need to have food and water and such things if they're going to travel a long way, don't they? What else do you think they might carry?'

Ben and Jess looked at each other, then Jess said that they might need a map and maybe a torch.

'I know,' Ben shouted. 'We can use my new backpack and fill it up with everything we need. I had a new torch as well. We'll have to make a map, though. Can you draw that, Jess? You're better than me at drawing.'

Jess nodded and sat at the table to start the map. Ben fetched his backpack and checked that the torch batteries were working. Gran put two bottles of water on the table and asked Ben what they would like to take to eat.

'Can we have some cheese sandwiches, please? Jess likes those best and so do I.'

So Gran made the sandwiches, wrapped them up and put them in the backpack. She also put in some chocolate biscuits and an apple for each of them.

'Now, find your boots and coats,' Gran said.

'Wait a minute, Ben.' Jess pulled on his sleeve. 'We've forgotten the magic wand. You know, the silver one that the dragon gave to the boy so that he could save the castle from the wizards from the dark lake.'

Ben looked at his gran. 'I'd forgotten that. Can you make some, Gran?'

Gran thought for a moment. 'What did you do with those balloons from your party, Ben? There were a few that were tied to sticks. We could use two of those if you can find them.'

Ben ran upstairs and picked up two of the balloons from the floor. He took them back to the kitchen and Gran cut the balloons off. Then she covered the sticks with silver foil.

'There you are, then. Two silver magic wands.' Gran handed them one each, then helped them with their coats and boots.

Scoot had been watching them very carefully and he was running around the kitchen in circles. He wanted to play as well. Gran said that he could go with them but only for a short time; otherwise she would have to bath him as well tonight! Ben took Scoot's whistle with him and he said he would show Jess how clever Scoot was.

# 5

## *Following The Magpies*

Ben and Jess and Scoot ran around the garden for some time, then Ben opened the shed door and pulled out two garden chairs. He sat down and called to Jess to do the same. They ate half of their sandwiches and one chocolate biscuit each, and drank some water. Ben filled Scoot's water bowl and he had a long drink too. Ben showed Jess how Scoot's whistle worked and she patted the dog's head. She thought he was a very clever dog and she wished she had one as well.

After they had played with Scoot they thought they would go back to the exploring game.

'Where did I put my magic wand, Jess?' Ben asked. He looked in his backpack, under the chair, inside the shed and on the path but he couldn't see it anywhere.

Jess pulled at his sleeve. He looked at her and saw that she had her finger over her mouth. She wanted him to be quiet, but why? Jess let go of his sleeve and pointed up at the roof of the house. Ben's mouth opened in surprise. Sitting on the roof were the two magpies he had seen that morning. He was sure it was the same pair. They were arguing again but not

about a piece of bread this time. No, they were fighting over something shiny. Something that Ben knew was his. It was the magic wand! The magpies must have taken it from somewhere in the garden.

'What shall we do, Ben?' Jess whispered. 'They're going to fly off with it, aren't they?'

'Yes, if we can't make them drop it first. Let's clap our hands and shout at them.' Ben puffed out his cheeks.

So Jess and Ben clapped and shouted, and Scoot barked, but the magpies ignored them. Then one flew off towards the woods carrying the wand. The other bird followed. Ben ran to the gate in the hedge but then he lost sight of the two birds and he stamped his foot hard.

'That's not fair! They're always taking things that don't belong to them. Now what are we going to do?' he shouted.

Jess caught up with him. 'Never mind, Ben. You can have my wand, or maybe your gran can make another one. What did you mean when you said that the magpies are always stealing? What else have they taken? You've never said anything about it before.'

Ben bit his lip. Should he tell Jess now about Lox and the spider gate? Maybe she could help him. He didn't think he could do it on his own any more. So they went back to the chairs and sat down, and Ben told Jess the whole story.

When he had finished, Jess looked at him and screwed up her nose.

'Are you making this up, Ben? Is this another one of your computer games or story books?' she asked.

'No! Really and truly,' Ben said. 'That's what happened. If we're very quiet I can show you the cave in the hedge but we have to be careful not to scare Lox or any of the other guards who might be there.'

Jess followed Ben to the bottom of the garden and they crawled under the hedge even though it was very wet on the ground. Jess saw the cave, and two big garden spiders just inside the opening, but she still wasn't sure if she believed Ben.

'Please, Jess, will you help me?' Ben said. 'I think I know where the magpies might have taken the other piece of the gate but I need to go outside to find it. Will you come?'

Jess looked worried. She knew they weren't allowed to go outside the garden on their own, but Ben was so upset and she really wanted to help her best friend. She knew that Ben's dad always bolted the gate in the hedge so she thought that they might not be able to open it anyway.

'All right, Ben.' Jess smiled at him. 'I'll help you but we have to put Scoot back in first. Remember what your gran said.'

'Yes, you're right. I'll take him in and say that we want to stay out a little bit longer.'

Ben called Scoot and the dog followed him to the kitchen door. Ben pulled off his boots, opened the door and went into the kitchen. Scoot followed him and went straight to his biscuit bowl. Ben looked for his gran and saw that she was in the living room reading the newspaper. Then he looked a little closer and saw that she was asleep. He didn't wake her. He shut Scoot in the kitchen, then put his boots back on and hurried down the path to Jess.

'Let's go,' he said. 'We have to open the gate first. If I bring a chair down here, I can stand on it and pull back the bolt.'

Jess just watched. She was scared but she didn't want to tell Ben. When he had opened the gate they went out into the lane.

'Do you think we should go back?' Jess asked. 'If we bolt the gate again no one will know. We're going to get into trouble if we stay out, aren't we?'

Ben looked at her. 'I know but if we can find the piece of the spider gate quickly we can be back before anyone knows. We won't stay out too long, I promise, but I have to try to find it.'

# 6

## *The Woods*

Jess followed Ben along the lane to the path that led into the woods. They walked for a long way. She didn't like it here. Even though lots of the leaves had come down from the trees it was still quite dark. She knew that her mum would be so cross with her, but Ben was unhappy about the missing piece of gate and she wanted to help him. He seemed so sure of where he was going. He said that his dad had brought him here in the summer with Scoot, and had shown him where the magpies built their nests. Ben thought that the birds might still come to the same place and maybe it was where they brought all the shiny things that they stole.

Jess wasn't sure if Ben really remembered the way. She decided that she would only go as far as the big holly bush just ahead of them. After that the bushes were thicker and the path was narrower, and Jess did not want to go there.

Ben switched on his torch and shone it on the ground as they walked along. He told Jess what to look for and they moved forward slowly. When they reached the holly bush, Jess stopped.

'Ben, I want to go back now. I don't like it here.'
She began to shake.

Ben stared at her and shook his head. 'Look,
Jess. Just there.' He shone the torch beam at a tree
just a little way further down the path. 'Can you
see them? The magpies are there. Right near the
top.'

Jess looked up and saw the two birds. They were
sitting side by side on a branch. They weren't arguing
any more and they seemed to be watching the torch
beam. Ben crept forward until he was underneath the
tree. He shone the torch all around the tree trunk and
kicked the fallen leaves with his boot.

'Jess! Jess! I've found the wand.' He picked it up
and waved it at her. 'I'm sure that the other piece of
gate must be here somewhere. Come on. Come and
help me find it.'

So Jess and Ben found some broken sticks and
prodded and poked all around the tree. The two
magpies watched them. Then Ben moved on to the
next tree and began again. Jess looked up at the sky
and saw some big black clouds. She knew that it was
going to start raining very soon.

'Come on, Ben. It's no good. You won't find
anything here and it's starting to rain. I want to go
back now. Please.'

Ben looked up. He could see that Jess was nearly
crying. He felt sorry that he'd asked her to come this
far. It was his task to find the last piece of the gate;
he was the one who had promised Lox. But he knew
Jess couldn't go back on her own, so he threw down
his stick.

'It's all right, Jess.' He smiled at her. 'We'll go now. Sorry.'

They began to walk back along the path but as they passed the tree where the magpies were sitting, Ben suddenly gave a shout.

Jess turned around but she couldn't see Ben anywhere. 'Ben! Ben! Where are you? Don't mess about, Ben. It's not fair. If you don't stop hiding right now, I'm going back without you. Can you hear me?'

Jess thought she could hear Ben laughing but she wasn't sure. She didn't think anything was funny. She meant what she had said about going back but she didn't know if she could find the way. She sat down on the ground and really began to cry. Big fat raindrops fell from the sky and hit her on the head. As she pulled up the hood of her coat, she saw Ben's torch lying next to the tree trunk. She picked it up and shone it around her.

'Ben? Ben!' Jess called again and again. She was frightened now. Ben wouldn't have left his torch if he was just hiding. 'Ben. Please tell me where you are.'

Then she heard a noise. Ben was calling her but she couldn't tell where the sound was coming from. She shone the torch around again and saw the silver wand poking out from under a large bramble bush. She knelt down and looked through the brambles. Ben was lying on his side. His face was scratched and bleeding and he had a big bump on his forehead.

'Ben! Are you all right? What happened?' Jess used the wand to hold the brambles back so that she could talk to Ben.

Ben groaned. 'I caught my foot in something and

rolled under here. I'm all scratched and I bumped my head and my foot hurts really badly. I've lost my boot as well. I don't think I can get out, Jess.'

Jess looked around. 'If I can find something to hold up the brambles, do you think you could slide out?'

'I don't know. It hurts so much.' Ben tried not to cry but the pain was so bad. He wished he was home in his warm bed.

Jess took the torch and tried to find some branches. There were a few near the tree trunk and a few more back along the path. She didn't really want to go off on her own but she knew that if she didn't help Ben to slide out from under the bramble bush, they could be in the woods for a long time. Jess did not want to be there when it got dark.

'Here.' Jess shone the torch in Ben's face and he blinked. 'Look, I've found some branches. I've pushed them under the brambles and I'll hold them up as far as I can. You try to crawl under them.'

Jess pulled the sleeves of her coat down over her hands and caught hold of the brambles. She pulled hard. Ben pushed himself up onto his elbows and began to crawl forwards very slowly and then he stopped.

'I can't do it, Jess. The brambles are still too low. They're going to cut my face again.' He laid his head on the ground.

'Pull your hood over your head,' Jess told him. 'Then pull it right down over your face. Just keep crawling towards me and you'll soon be out.'

So Ben did what Jess had said and very slowly he crawled out. Then he lay on the path. Jess sat down next to him. They were both very tired and the rain was pouring down. They knew that they should try to get back to Ben's house but he couldn't stand up. His foot was very swollen.

'What are we going to do, Ben?' Jess asked. 'We can't stay here all night.'

'It's all right. Dad will find us, I bet.'

Ben hoped this was true but he didn't even know when his mum and dad would be home. He looked around and saw how dark it was becoming, and he knew that he had made a big mistake.

# 7

## *Scoot's Search*

When Ben's grandmother woke up she knew that something was wrong. She could hear Scoot barking in the kitchen and she could see that it was raining again. She opened the door and the dog ran around whining and jumping up at her.

'What's the matter, Scoot? Where's Ben?' Gran looked into the kitchen but the light was off. She thought that Ben and Jess might be playing on the computer so she went into the dining room but there was no one there. Upstairs was also quiet so she went out into the garden. Perhaps they were in the shed? It was now raining very heavily.

'Ben! Jess! Are you there?' Gran called, but no one answered. She was really worried, so she put on her raincoat and went down the garden path. When she saw the chair and the open gate she was very afraid. She looked up and down the lane but there was no sign of Ben or Jess. She called and called to them but there was no answer, so she ran back to the house and telephoned Ben's dad and told him what had happened.

Half an hour later, Ben's mother and father arrived

home. Ben's dad put on his boots and his big raincoat. He found his torch and then told Ben's mum to telephone Jess's mother. He called for Scoot and then they went through the gate into the lane.

'Good boy, Scoot. Find Ben. Find Ben.'

Scoot wagged his tail and ran around. First he went up the lane and then he came back down, sniffing the ground and the grass at the sides. After a few moments he lifted his head up and trotted down the lane towards the woods.

'Oh no,' Dad groaned. 'Not the woods. Come on Scoot, before it gets too dark.'

They hurried down the path but when they came to the place where the path split into two they didn't know which way to go. Scoot looked up and down and then ran off to the right. Dad followed. All of a sudden Scoot stopped. He lifted up his head and began to shake.

'What is it, boy?' Dad asked. 'What can you hear?'

Scoot looked up at him, then turned around and ran back to the other path. He began to run faster, and Ben's dad ran after him.

Ben and Jess were cold and very tired. Jess didn't think that anyone would find them so Ben was trying to think of some way to stop her from crying. He told her stories and he even told her what his birthday wish had been. He didn't care now. It was almost too late to save the spider gate anyway.

'What are we going to say, Ben? When everyone asks us why we came here?' Jess asked.

Ben thought for a moment. 'If we tell them we were following the magpies so that we could look for the spider gate piece, they'll say we're being silly. The magpies did steal the magic wand though, so we could say that's why we came here.'

Jess frowned. She didn't want to tell a lie but the magpies really had taken the wand, so she just nodded. She was looking sad again so Ben started to tell her more about Scoot's training. Then he remembered that he still had the whistle.

'Jess! The whistle is in my pocket. If you can reach it, then Scoot can find us if Dad brings him out. Please try.'

Jess pulled the whistle out and blew it really hard. She kept blowing for a few minutes, then Ben tried. They took turns until they were both dizzy.

'It's no good, Ben,' Jess moaned. 'No one's coming.'

Then they heard a crashing noise and barking and shouting. Suddenly Ben's dad was there and Scoot was jumping all over them and licking them and wagging his tail. Dad picked Ben up and told Jess to hold onto his coat.

Back at Ben's house everyone was waiting for them. Jess's mum was crying and Ben's mum and his gran were looking very worried. Dad laid Ben down on

the settee and his mum took off his coat. Gran and Jess's mum took off Jess's coat and then washed her face and hands.

Gran found a tracksuit and T shirt of Ben's for Jess, as her clothes were so wet. When she was dry, Gran made her some hot milk and then Jess's mum took her home. Her mother had not told her off yet, but Jess knew that she was in big trouble and tomorrow she would have to try to explain why she had gone outside the garden.

After Jess had gone, Ben's dad thought that he should take Ben to the hospital. The bump on his forehead was very big and his foot was hurting him a lot. So his mum wrapped him in a blanket and Dad carried him out to the car.

'Be brave, Ben,' Gran told him as they were going out of the door.

Ben lifted up his head. 'Sorry, Gran. I didn't mean to frighten you.'

'I know you didn't,' Gran told him, 'but we don't have time to talk now. You can tell me all about it tomorrow.'

# 8

## *The Final Piece*

The next morning when Ben woke up, he was hurting all over. He tried to sit up but he felt so sick that he lay down again. He pushed back the duvet and looked at his foot. The doctor at the hospital had said that it wasn't broken but that Ben should rest it. The nurse had cleaned it and then put a big bandage on it. Ben felt the bump on his forehead. It was very sore. The doctor said that it was just a bruise but that it would hurt for a week. Ben couldn't see the scratches on his face but they were still stinging.

He settled back down in his bed. It was early and no one was moving in the house. He felt very sleepy but he was so worried about what his mum and dad were going to say to him today. They had told him the night before how glad they were that he was safe, but Ben knew he had done something wrong and he was going to be in trouble about it. He was worried about Lox too, and the last piece of the gate. The doctor had said that Ben needed to stay in bed for at least four days. Ben counted on his fingers.

'Today is Sunday. So that's Monday, Tuesday, Wednesday.'

He also knew that he wouldn't be able to put on his shoes or to walk properly for ages, and that meant he couldn't go outside. It was hopeless. He'd never find the missing piece. His head was aching now and he felt very hot. He turned towards the window but he couldn't see out because the curtains were closed. He shut his eyes and after a while he went back to sleep – he dreamed about magpies and pieces of the spider gate and dragons. Just at the moment when the dragon was going to take the last piece of the gate from the magpies, Ben's mother came into his room and he woke up.

'Good morning, Ben. How are you feeling today?' she asked.

Ben rubbed his eyes. 'My head hurts.'

'I'm not surprised,' Mum said. 'You have a really big bump. Now, let me help you to sit up and you can have your breakfast in bed. I'll help you to wash, and to clean your teeth later, and then Dad and you need to have a talk.'

Ben began to cry. 'I'm sorry, Mum. I know I shouldn't have gone out.'

His mum smiled at him. 'Don't get upset, Ben. I'm sure you and Dad will be able to sort things out. I was very cross with you last night but I'm just glad that Scoot found you and that you weren't hurt too badly.'

Later that morning Ben thought about everything that had happened. He had told his dad about the magpies and the wand and how he had opened the gate. He said that it was his fault and that Jess only went along because he asked her to. Dad said he was putting a lock on the gate and that Ben was not to try to go out alone again until he was older. Dad promised to take Ben and Scoot out for training on Saturday mornings if it wasn't raining. He said that when Ben was better he would have to help Gran and Mum for two weeks with extra jobs around the house. He would also have to help Dad to clear up the leaves from the garden and he couldn't play on the computer for a month.

On Thursday Ben was allowed out of bed. His mum pushed a chair near the bedroom window so that he could look out. She gave him a book and told him that Gran would come up soon to help him read it. Ben put the book down and looked at the big trees at the bottom of the garden. He could see that lots of the leaves had fallen off and most of the others were yellow or brown. There were only a few that were still green. He felt very sad.

'Cheer up, Mister Grumpy!' Gran sat down on the end of the bed. 'What's the matter?'

Ben looked up. 'Hello, Gran. I was just looking at the leaves. I don't like it when they fall off.'

Gran patted his hand. 'Never mind. There will be plenty more next year. Now, what about that book?'

'I don't really want to read. Can you just tell me a story? Tell me about when you were little.' Ben smiled at his gran. He knew she liked to talk about when she was growing up, but he liked the stories as well.

'If that's what you want, Ben. You remember that I used to live in this house when I was your age, don't you? The trees in the garden weren't quite so big then and the hedge wasn't there at all. My father planted it when I was eight years old. I used to go out all the time to see how much it was growing. I would lie on the ground and stare at the bushes for hours. One day I fell asleep in the garden and had a very strange dream.'

Ben sat up. 'What dream, Gran? Why haven't you told me this story before?'

Gran smiled. 'I don't know. Anyway, I dreamed I was tiny and that I was talking to ladybirds and all sorts of creatures, then I woke up. It's funny how I forgot that until now. It must have been your story about the boy in the garden that reminded me.'

Ben looked at Gran closely. She was staring out of the window and smiling.

'Oh, Ben. I nearly forgot.' Gran put her hand into her pocket. 'Your coat was so ripped from the brambles that we had to throw it away but this was caught in the lining. I don't know what it is but I thought you might want it.' She opened her fist and on the palm of her hand was a tiny parcel wrapped up in silver foil.

Ben took the parcel. He unwrapped it carefully and there, sitting in a little nest of tissue paper, was the third piece of the spider gate. Ben was so surprised that he nearly dropped it.

'Was I right?' Gran asked him. 'You do want it?'

Ben looked at her and nodded. Gran stood up and said she had to go the shops. As she opened the door

47

she turned around and said, 'You take good care of that now. Looks like a real piece of treasure to me. You and Jess are certainly good explorers. I'll see you later. Maybe you can finish that story for me soon?' Then she winked at him and left.

Ben turned the piece of gate over and over in his hand. What did Gran mean? Did she really have a dream in the garden or had she become small just like Ben had? Maybe Gran had seen the spider gate before it was broken. Ben didn't know how long it had been there. He didn't think Lox had said, but that didn't matter now. Ben was worried that he wouldn't be able to go out into the garden in time. He would have to think of some way to give Lox the final piece of the gate.

# 9

## *The Spider Wizard's Magic*

Two days later, on Saturday, Ben's dad helped him downstairs onto the settee. Ben could walk a little bit now but his foot was still sore. He watched television for a while, then Mum helped him into the kitchen.

'Time to eat something, Ben.' Gran told him. 'We have to build up your strength before you go back to school.'

Ben had missed a whole week of school. He hoped he would be well enough to go back on Monday, but he had to wait to see what the doctor said. He wondered how Jess was. He hoped she hadn't been told off too much.

'Mum,' Ben asked, 'is Jess all right? Have you heard from her mother? She will be allowed to play with me again, won't she?'

'Don't worry,' Mum said. 'Her mother is bringing her over this afternoon for an hour. She can tell you what you've missed in school. Gran found some cards in the drawer this morning so you can play with those if you like.'

Jess arrived at half past two and her mother said she would come back after she had done her ironing.

Ben's mum and dad had gone to the shops and Gran was in the kitchen baking cakes. Jess told Ben all about the models they were making in school and about the drawing she had done of a castle and a dragon. Then Ben pulled the piece of the spider gate from his pocket.

'Look, Jess. It's the last piece. Gran found it stuck in my coat. It must have been under the bramble bush all the time.'

Jess opened her eyes wide and put her hand over her mouth. 'That's great, Ben, but how are you going to put it under the hedge if you can't walk properly? Your mum and dad won't let you go out by yourself yet will they?'

'No, I don't think so,' Ben said, 'but you could do it, Jess. You know where the cave is and it wouldn't take you long. You'd only have to put the piece next to the cave and just leave it there. I wanted to see them put the gate back together again, but we'll know the next time we look if the Spider Wizard fixed it, won't we? I'm sorry I won't be able to see Lox again, but maybe next year, when the summer holidays come again, I might try to find him. Will you do it, Jess?'

Jess wasn't sure. She didn't want to get into trouble again. She'd had to go to bed early every night last week and she wasn't allowed to watch television at all for two weeks. She asked Ben, 'What about your gran? Won't she stop me from going out?'

Ben shook his head. 'I think she already knows about the gate but I'm not sure. Anyway, she's just gone upstairs so if you're quick you can be back before she comes down.'

Jess took the piece of gate and held it on her hand. She touched it with her finger. 'It's really pretty, Ben. Maybe I could have it as a charm for my bracelet.'

Ben's face went red, but before he could say anything Jess said she was only joking. She ran into the kitchen and opened the door quietly. She ran down the path and knelt down next to the hedge at the back of the garden. She remembered the spot where Ben had shown her the spider cave and she placed the last piece of the gate carefully on the ground. She waited for a moment but nothing happened so she stood up and ran back to the house.

'I did it, Ben. I did it,' she said as she sat down next to him. Her cheeks were red and she looked pleased with herself.

'Thanks, Jess.' Ben smiled at her. 'It's up to Lox now. We can't do any more.'

Two weeks later, when Ben was much better and was able to walk on his own, he went back to school. Jess asked him if the spider gate was fixed but he told her that he hadn't been able to go into the garden yet. Jess hadn't been able to visit him after the day she'd put the last piece of the gate back, because she'd had a cold and her mother had made her stay in the house.

'I'll have to wait for Saturday,' Ben told Jess, 'because it's too dark now after school. I hope it doesn't rain.'

Jess groaned. It was such a long time until

Saturday. She really wanted to be with Ben when he looked but she didn't know if he'd ask her. Then he said, 'If your mother will let you come over on Saturday, we can look together, if you like.'

Jess grinned. 'Oh, yes, please!'

They were both happy when Saturday morning turned out bright and sunny, but it was very cold. Ben's mum had picked up Jess, and at eleven o'clock Jess and Ben were sitting at the kitchen table drinking milk and eating some of Gran's little cakes. Ben's dad was in the shed mending one of the bird feeders. Ben opened the back door and called to him.

'Dad! Dad! Can we come out and play with Scoot?'

His dad came out of the shed and looked at the sky. 'Yes, all right then, but only for half an hour. It's cold today. Ask Gran to help you to wrap up warmly.'

Jess and Ben did as they were told and they were soon throwing a ball for Scoot to chase. Scoot was very excited and ran round and round, barking and wagging his tail. Ben threw the ball towards the gate and watched as it rolled underneath the hedge. He looked at Jess and they both ran after Scoot who was chasing the ball.

'Shall we look now, Jess?' Ben asked. 'It's the best chance we have. I put my torch in my pocket so we can see properly. Are you ready?'

Jess was too excited to talk so she just nodded. Ben pulled out the ball and threw it so that Scoot would

run back up the garden. He knelt down and switched on the torch. Jess knelt down beside him. They looked at each other and then Ben pushed the torch right under the hedge.

At first they couldn't see anything. It seemed as though the cave had disappeared. Then Ben nudged Jess and said, 'Look! Right at the back by the big stone.'

Jess looked and gasped. The torch beam was shaking but they could both see something shining in the light. It was there. It was in one piece. The spider gate had been fixed. Ben wasn't sure but he thought he could see something moving behind the gate. Maybe it was Lox. Maybe it was just a shadow.

Ben and Jess walked slowly back up the garden path. They didn't want to play ball any more. They wanted to talk about what they'd just seen. As they passed the garden shed Ben looked up to his bedroom window and saw his gran waving to him. She smiled and she winked at him.

Ben waved back. Maybe Gran really did know everything!

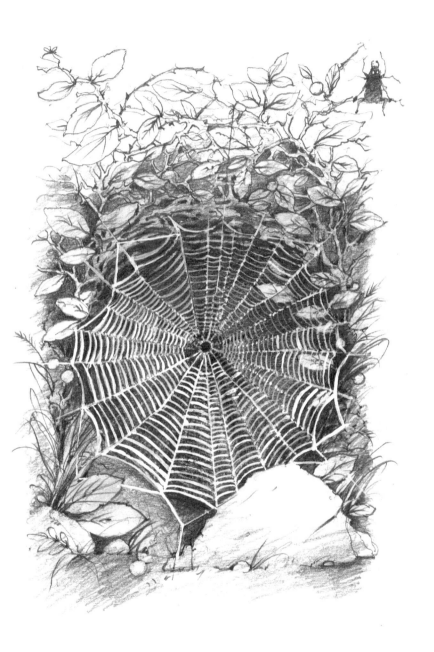

## Ben's Birthday Wish Rhyme

Red, orange, yellow,
green, purple, blue.
Please make my birthday
wish come true.

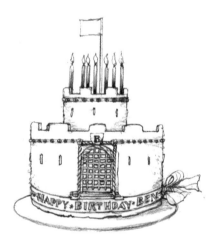

# Ben and the Spider Prince

Lox and the Spider Wizard need Ben's help again, but can Ben find the special ingredients in time to make the magic potion to cure the Spider Prince's illness? Will Gran tell Ben a secret that will keep him safe from Spindra, the evil sister of the Spider Queen?

'Now then,' Gran said, 'what's this important thing you want to talk about?'

Ben wriggled in his seat. 'Do you remember the story that I told you last year about the spider gate and the magpies?' Gran nodded her head. 'Well, it wasn't a story. It really happened. I don't know how I became small. I just fell asleep in the garden and when I woke up I was little! You do believe me, don't you?'

Gran patted his hand. 'Of course I do. I knew all along.'

Ben's mouth fell open. 'How did you know? Why didn't you say anything?'

'Slow down.' Gran laughed out loud. 'I have a

lot to tell you, but you must promise to keep it a secret.'

Find out more in April 2016